T0365911

Minnie Mornap
TEEN REPORTER

D.W. Paone

authorHOUSE®

AuthorHouse™
1663 Liberty Drive
Bloomington, IN 47403
www.authorhouse.com
Phone: 1 (800) 839-8640

Front and back cover photographs by Liz & Joe Schmidt
Photography, Rockville Centre, New York.

Published by AuthorHouse   11/10/2016

ISBN: 978-1-5246-4547-2 (sc)
ISBN: 978-1-5246-4546-5 (e)

Library of Congress Control Number: 2016917344

Print information available on the last page.

For C.M.G.

Chapter One

Minnie Mornap awoke to think, "What will today bring?" And by today she didn't mean just today, but the whole year, because today is the first day of school for Succotash Central High. In fact, it's the first day of school for the entire Succotash Central School District.

If the suburbs are the link between the city and the country, then Succotash is the link between the country and the suburbs. Succotash has a "downtown," with a mall and car dealerships and everything any suburban downtown would have, but it also has farms with real-live cows.

If you were to view the place from up above, it would look something like a bull's eye. Downtown is the center circle, then the houses of the development making the next larger circle and finally the farms making the biggest circle.

The place covers a lot of ground so getting from one end to the other takes a lot of time. For the kids who live on the farms, the bus ride to school each day begins during the dark hour of the morning.

It seems most of everyone's time is spent driving. Ever since middle school all of Minnie's friends couldn't wait to drive. Not just because it's fun to drive without your parents, but it was more like a necessity. Up until 16 everyone has to depend on someone else to get around.

This is why everyone's parents own an SUV. One owns an actual 12-seat, passenger van. Carpools are big in Succotash. Almost every trip includes a neighbor or two. Sometimes Minnie would wonder how anyone got around here before SUVs. She quickly deduced that's what station wagons were for.

That's how Minnie's mind works. Quick deductions. She inherited this trait from her father. Her father is a lawyer. Whenever she hears snide comments about lawyers — how untrustworthy they are — she can never quite understand. Her father is very trustworthy. And it's his deductive reasoning and use of logic that she admires the most.

He puts it this way: "If people did the logical thing, there'd be no lawsuits. Say it snows. The logical thing is to shovel your walk. But say you don't shovel your walk and the snow turns to ice? And someone slips and hurts himself? What can we deduce? There would be no injury if you did the logical thing and if I can prove you *didn't* do the logical thing, then I will win the lawsuit. It's that simple."

Mr. Mornap is only half of the law firm of Mornap & Turner. Mr. Turner, the other lawyer, is more like the lawyers people love to hate. He's what they call an "ambulance chaser."

He really doesn't care who his clients are or what their cases are about; he's more interested in quick money to be made in settlements. In an effort to counteract this, Mr. Mornap is also the public defender in the area.

That means poor people who are accused of a crime, who cannot afford a lawyer, have Mr. Mornap represent them. He doesn't get paid a lot for this work and most of the people he represents are guilty of their crimes (and everyone knows it) but he still does a good job as their lawyer.

Minnie doesn't pay much mind to what goes on at Mornap & Turner. She has another connection with the firm which is a bit indirect. She's best friends with Mr. Turner's daughter, Tracy. Minnie and Tracy Turner have been best friends since kindergarten. And when you're friends for that long, it really doesn't matter what your fathers do.

***

After trying on three outfits Minnie decides on the first one. Being an only child she has her own room and never has to wear hand-me-downs.

After breakfast she, her father and her mother venture out to the shiny, black SUV in the driveway. The routine has been the same for years. Her parents drop her off at school and then continue on to her father's office.

Her mother is the receptionist so it's no problem for her to leave in the afternoon to pick Minnie up from school. On the rare occasion Minnie is sick, Mrs. Mornap can take the entire day off to stay home with her.

This hasn't happened in a long time. Today is the start of Minnie's sophomore year and so far she has perfect attendance in high school.

Part of the routine she dreads. They drive down the block to pick up Eddie Hanson. Eddie is in Minnie's class and she can't stand him. He's the kind of boy who sticks pencils up his nose and thinks it's hilarious.

Unfortunately, all the other boys in the class think it's hilarious, too, and this encourages Eddie to stick more things up his nose.

Minnie has very little use for boys. Here's how she came to that conclusion:

1. Boys are immature.
2. The things boys like (video games, wrestling) she doesn't, and
3. The things she likes (museums, dance recitals) they don't, therefore
4. We can conclude boys have no real use.

Now this isn't entirely true. Minnie has a cousin, Neil. He's a lifetime older than she is (21) and goes to college and is in a band (which is really awful but that doesn't matter, it's a *band*) and on the weekends he's a bartender at a club. Not a restaurant, but a club. Minnie isn't sure what the difference is, but a club sounds a whole lot cooler for some reason.

And while she never saw him perform this job, she's sure he's not doing it with pencils hanging out of his nose.

Yes, Neil is cool. Why can't Eddie be like Neil? Why can't all the boys at Succotash Central be like Neil? If they were, then she'd have some use for them.

Mrs. Mornap pulls up in front of Eddie's house. And there's Eddie waiting for her — with pencils hanging out of his nose. Minnie can only turn away in disgust. Eddie climbs in.

"Hi, Minnie!"

Eddie, with pencils dangling, waits for a laugh that doesn't come.

***

The drive to school seemed eternal but Minnie survived. Before the car came to a complete stop Minnie was unbuckled and out the door. Now where is Tracy?

Tracy is flirting with Bobby Taylor. The only problem is, Bobby doesn't know he's being flirted with. Boys can be so clueless sometimes. This is very frustrating for Tracy.

Minnie arrives just as Tracy twirls her hair.

"Here you are," Minnie says to Tracy. "I hope I'm not interrupting anything."

"Unfortunately, you're not," laments Tracy. "Let's go." As Minnie and Tracy step away, Bobby says, "See you later!"

"Sure," says Tracy, with a roll of her eyes.

Minnie produces her schedule. "What do you have first?"

"Um... chemistry. How about you?"

"Journalism," replies Minnie. "Shouldn't be too bad. May even be fun." The first bell rings. "I guess I'll find out now."

***

As Minnie walks to class, looking at the numbers on the classroom doors, she feels a little afraid. There is no reason to be afraid, she deduces, freshman year is long over and there's nothing more freighting than being a freshman. So what's the problem?

The problem is the unknown can be scary even when it shouldn't be. Yes, the class could very well be fun, but it could be just awful, too.

***

Mr. Hecht stands before the class. He's kind of old, even for a teacher. Gray hair, a receding hairline and just enough lines to give his face character. He wears a wrinkled sports jacket and a tie whose knot hangs a good two inches from his unbuttoned collar. Blue jeans and sneakers complete this ensemble, making him appear slightly more youthful than he really is.

He gives the class a good looking over before he speaks. The late bell echoes throughout the building. This is his cue to start.

"This is a journalism class. That makes you journalists. And I don't mean a journal like a diary or a 'blog' or whatever it's called these days — I mean an old-fashioned newspaper. Your job is to put out a newspaper every four weeks. Now the first thing is you have to start looking, sounding and acting like newspaper people.

"So first thing tomorrow everyone shows up with coffee. And I don't mean a latte or some other pansy coffee drink; I mean a cup of mud from a gas station or some 24-hour joint where they never clean the pots! And God help you if you don't drink it black. By Christmas I expect everyone to have a caffeine addiction. Oh, and from here on in everyone calls me Chief."

Was this guy for real? Or was this just some theatrics to get the class going? No one could tell.

"When I call your name, tell me what you may want to write about in the paper." He looks at the roster. "Ambrico, Christina."

Christina Ambrico surely doesn't want to go first, but with the name Ambrico, she goes first all the time.

"Uh... I like to write poetry."

"Poetry!? Save that for the literary magazine, sweetheart. We're here to write news." He looks at the roster again. "Bence, Laura."

"Sports?"

"Was that a question or a statement? Sure, every newspaper has a sports section. That's more like it." He reads the next name. "Damm, Morton. *Morton*?" The class laughs.

9

"Yes, Mr. Hecht."

Mr. Hecht gives him a look.

"I mean Chief. I like to take pictures."

"Pictures are terrific! Every newspaper needs pictures. Do you know what a newspaper without pictures is? *Reader's Digest,* that's what!" He reads the next name. "Hearst, Justin. *Hearst?*"

"That's me, Chief," says one boy.

"I gotta ask."

"Yes, William Randolph Hearst was my grandfather's uncle."

"Here is your first homework assignment. Watch *Citizen Kane.*" He writes "Citizen Kane" on the board.

"It's old, long and in black and white, but you'll have a peek into the life of one of the biggest names in publishing. Charles Foster Kane is a thinly disguised version of William Randolph Hearst, whose legacy in journalism continues today. As for you, you have some pretty big shoes to fill."

"I know, Chief. But I can fill them. I guarantee it. After all, journalism is in my blood."

"Confident, are we?" asks Mr. Hecht rhetorically. "What do you want to write about?"

"The human condition."

"I'll just ignore that." He reads the next name. "Mornap, Minnie."

"Investigative reporting," Minnie says with little hesitation.

"Ah... investigative reporting... my favorite type of journalism!" exclaims Mr. Hecht.

"I meant to say that, Chief! It just came out wrong," interjects Justin.

"You meant to say 'investigative reporting' and it came out 'the human condition'?"

"Uh... yeah."

"I see. After everyone watches *Citizen Kane*, your next assignment is to read *All the President's Men*. It's investigative reporting at its best. If the written word can bring down the president of the United States, then it can do anything."

Justin glances over at Minnie with a look of contempt. She doesn't know it yet, but she has made an enemy.

Chapter Two

The class files in. Each student holds a cup of coffee purchased minutes before. Mr. Hecht eyes each cup as it passes before him, nodding with approval. Until he sees what Justin is holding.

"What in the name of Hildy Johnson is that?" he asks.

Justin has a carton in his hands, which he places on a random desk. He pulls out its content, one item at a time. The first is a coffeemaker.

"Since you want us to drink coffee, Chief, I thought I'd make that easy to do. Here's everything we need. A coffeemaker, coffee, filters, cups, sugar... I brought stirrers, too."

Mr. Hecht doesn't know whether to be thrilled or insulted. Thrilled because it's a great idea but insulted because it's an obvious ploy by Justin to get in his good graces. After a moment of debate he says, "Capital idea! Set it up in the corner."

Justin looks over at Minnie for approval, but she just rolls her eyes. Morton takes a seat next to Minnie. Justin gets busy setting up his new toy.

"Can you believe this guy?" whispers Morton to Minnie.

"Well, it's better than sticking pencils up his nose," she whispers back.

"What?"

"Never mind."

The late bell rings. "OK, staff, today we're going to start with our basic question, 'What is news?'"

He gestures towards the board, where that very question is written near the top.

"There are two types of news, hard and soft."

He writes "Hard" and "Soft" on the board, creating two columns under the question.

"Someone name a subject that we read about in the paper everyday." A girl raises her hand. "Yes."

"Politics?"

"Absolutely!"

Underneath the word "Hard," Mr. Hecht writes "Politics."

"In the school environment, politics will include anything with administration. Just as the governor runs the state, the superintendent runs the district. What else?"

A boy says, "The arts?"

"Very good!" shouts Mr. Hecht.

Under "Soft" he writes, "The Arts."

"If a movie breaks a box office record, that's soft news. What else?"

Laura says, "Sports!"

"You and sports, again. I'm going to put 'Sports' in between because if the home team is having a so-so season, then it's soft news. But if they're undefeated or in the playoffs, then it's hard news.

"I'm also going to put 'The Weather' in the middle, too. If it snows six inches, it's soft news. If it snows six*teen* inches, it's hard news. Gimme more. Minnie, any ideas?"

"What if someone gets murdered?"

"Ah, murder! A reporter's favorite crime. From here on in we call it 'homicide.' Yes, homicide is always news. Why?"

The class is silent.

"It's something that shouldn't happen so when it does, people want to know the details. We can put a lot of things in the same category. Car accidents, assault, fires, robbery... anything where there's damage to people or property is hard news. The bigger the damage, the bigger the news."

He writes "Damage Stories" under hard news. He turns to Justin.

"Hey, Coffee Boy, is that thing set up yet?"

"Almost, Chief. I forgot the power cord." The class laughs. "I'll have it tomorrow, Chief!"

"For the remainder of today, I want everyone to come up with a possible article to write for our first issue. It can be hard news or it can be soft news. I want you to look around all day today.

"And I mean really *look*. And listen. What are the students doing? What are they talking about? What's on their minds? What work is being done on the building? What work *isn't* being done on the building but should be? First thing tomorrow we'll go around the room and see what you've come up with."

***

Minnie slowly walks to her next class as the rest of the school rushes past her. Her assignment is to look; so she's going to look. Her head turns left and right as she walks down the hall and the voice in her head assesses what she sees.

"There's a maintenance man fixing a doorknob. Is that hard news? Is that soft news? Is that news at all? I don't think so.

"There's a custodian with a mop and bucket. That's not news; it's just disgusting. Here's something! Someone is hanging a poster for our first pep rally of the year. Gee... not a lot of newsworthy events go on at this school."

***

"OK, whaddya got? Christina, you're up," says Mr. Hecht.

"Um... they mowed the lawn yesterday."

Mr. Hecht looks at her blankly. "Tell me, would you read an article about lawn mowing?"

"No, Chief," she timidly replies.

"No one would. Is that all you have?"

"Yes, Chief."

"Laura, hit me with something great."

"The girls' junior varsity soccer team got new uniforms." Mr. Hecht is a bit intrigued.

"Why?"

"Because most of the girls got fat over the summer."

"We can't write that! I mean, while some may consider that news, I'd only include that in a bigger story about childhood obesity or something. Anything else?"

"No, Chief."

"Here's your opportunity, Mr. Journal-ism-Is-In-My-Blood."

"I... didn't have a chance to do the assignment," confesses Justin.

"You had all day yesterday to look and come up with one idea. You 'didn't have a chance' to do *that*?" asks Mr. Hecht.

"I had... some personal problems yesterday."

"Personal problems?"

"Yeah. But I brought the power cord!" He holds up the cord and gives Mr. Hecht a big, toothy grin. Mr. Hecht turns to Minnie.

"Minnie?"

"The varsity cheerleading team put up posters for a pep rally next week. Is that news?"

"Is that news?!" shouts Mr. Hecht. "It certainly is. Finally, someone has a newsworthy idea. Halleluiah!"

Minnie certainly doesn't want to be the teacher's pet, but it's turning out that way. On the other hand, Justin is *dying* to be the teacher's pet and it's *not* turning out that way. He resents Minnie even more.

***

Minnie and Tracy sit at a table in the cafeteria. Morton approaches, holding his tray. "May I join you?"

"Sure," says Minnie. Morton takes a seat.

"I really like your pep rally idea."

"Oh, thanks."

"The only thing I came up with was a guy fixing a doorknob."

"I saw that, too!" exclaims Minnie. Morton is thrilled at this. Score one point in the "made-a-connection" column. He tries for another.

"Not a lot of newsworthy events go on at this school."

"That's what I said!" exclaims Minnie with even more enthusiasm.

Score! He tries for three.

"I bet the pep rally will be really dull," Morton states emphatically.

"I don't think so. We've had them before. They're not so bad."

Swing and a miss. Morton back peddles a bit.

"I'm sure you're right. We'll know next week."

***

Everyone sits with a cup of coffee and a handout on his desk.

"Today we're going to start with vocabulary used in journalism," says Mr. Hecht. "From here on in you're to use these words correctly. The words are on your handout; you fill in the definitions. The first word is 'copy.'

"In the publishing world, this doesn't mean a reproduction; 'copy' is the words on the paper. Write that down."

The class writes down, "Words on the paper."

"When I say, 'Have you handed in your copy?' I mean, 'Have you handed in your article?' So a 'copywriter' is the person who

writes copy. That's your second vocab word."
He waits a beat while they write.

"The next word is the most important word
in the business. 'Deadline.' A deadline is the last
possible minute you can hand in your copy or
your photograph or whatever it is you're going
to have in the paper. If you miss your deadline,
your work will not make the paper. Editors —
and journalism teachers — hate it when you
miss your deadline.

"A 'headline' is the title of an article. A
'byline' is who wrote the article. So we have
deadlines, headlines and bylines. Pretty easy
to remember.

"Some headlines have a smaller headline
underneath it to further explain the story. This
is called a 'dek.' He waits a beat for the class to
catch up.

"'Layout' is where the elements are put
on the page. 'Put to bed' means the paper is
finished being laid out and is ready to go to
the printer. At this point no changes can be
made. There will be a quiz on these words on
Thursday. Memorize them.

"Next, we're going to go over what questions
need to be answered in every article. Hard news,

soft news, sports... it doesn't matter... every article needs to answer these questions. Take notes."

He writes "Who, What, When" and "Where" on the board.

"*Who* is the article about? The varsity football team. *What* did they do? They were in the playoffs. *When* did it happen? On Friday, November 13th. Friday the 13th is always good for 'when.' *Where* did this happen? Right here at Succotash Central High School." Minnie raises her hand.

"Wouldn't that make every article four sentences long?"

"Excellent observation!" says Mr. Hecht. "Keep in mind our questions can be answered with more than one fact. Take our 'what.' It's not just they played the game, but what the score was. What the weather was. What the reaction of the crowd was. What the coach did. What the quarterback did. There are a lot of 'whats' to be answered."

He writes "Why" and "How" on the board.

"These next two questions you can't always answer or you don't need to answer. *Why* did the football team play the game? I think we all know why. *Why* was someone murdered?

"Sometimes we'll know right away and other times we won't ever know. *How* was he murdered? Again, sometimes we'll know right away and sometimes not. But if you can answer those questions as well, then that's even better. Next thing is —"

Just then two boys barge into the classroom. One wears a wizard hat and the other wears a top hat. One wears a baseball jersey and one wears a football jersey. Both hold bananas, pointed as guns.

They run up to Mr. Hecht and point the bananas at him. The first one says, "Give me your money!"

Mr. Hecht replies, "I don't have any money. I'm a poor teacher."

The second one says, "Then give us a cup of coffee."

Mr. Hecht says, "How do you take it?"

The first one says, "Black with one sugar," and the second one says, "Milk with two sugars."

Mr. Hecht walks over to the coffeemaker, pours the two cups as instructed and hands them to him the boys. The first one puts his banana down on Mr. Hecht's desk and they run out of the room.

No one knows what to make of this. What was that all about?

"OK, class," Mr. Hecht says. "I want everyone to write a short article on what just happened. Answer all the questions you can. And I'd like to thank David Edds and Ernie Labra from Mr. Taranto's drama class for their fine performances."

David and Ernie step back into the classroom and take a bow.

"You have 15 minutes. Start writing."

***

It was a long 15 minutes. Minnie did her best to remember all the facts. This journalism was harder than she thought.

"Let's hear whatcha got!" shouts Mr. Hecht.

"Christina, you're up first."

With great hesitation Christina reads her copy. "Two boys wearing hats and uniforms ran into the classroom...."

"What *kind* of hats, Christina? What *kind* of uniforms? Who can tell me what kind of hats they wore?" asks Mr. Hecht.

The class is silent. "No one noticed?"

The truth is Minnie noticed but was afraid to say so.

"One was pointy," says a girl.

"Pointy. Not exactly the answer I was looking for. Morton, read what happened next from your copy."

Morton knows his account is even worse than Laura's.

"Umm… One boy said, 'Give me your money,' and Mr. Hecht said, 'I have no money; I'm an underpaid teacher.'"

"Is that what I said, Morton? Not really."

Mr. Hecht falls silent as does the entire class. It's actually pretty creepy how silent it became all of a sudden. He looks up and down the rows, directly into the eyes of each student. They can tell he's not happy.

His gaze lands on Minnie. At long last the silence is broken when Mr. Hecht speaks again.

"Minnie, read yours from the top."

"Here goes," thinks Minnie. Not knowing what to expect, she begins reading.

"About half way through first period on Thursday, two boys wearing costumes barged into Mr. Hecht's classroom. One wore a wizard hat and baseball jersey and the other wore a top hat and football jersey. Both held bananas, pointed as guns.

"They ran up to Mr. Hecht and pointed the bananas at him. The first one said, 'Give me your money!' and Mr. Hecht replied, 'I don't have any money. I'm a poor teacher.'"

Mr. Hecht, as well as the rest of the class, can't believe what they're hearing.

"The second one said, 'Then give us a cup of coffee.' Mr. Hecht said, 'How do you take it?'"

Minnie looks up from her paper to see the entire class staring at her in silence. She turns her head left and then right. Yes, it's the entire class.

"Uh… I don't remember how they took their coffee. But I do remember one left a banana on your desk."

"Hallelujah!" shouts Mr. Hecht. "Finally, someone got something right! That is an excellent first try. Thank you, Minnie! Oh, and nice use of the word 'barged.' And notice she knows when to use 'as' instead of 'like.'"

Minnie doesn't like all this attention. Or at least that's what she tells herself. On the other hand, she really does like it. Perhaps she's a better journalist than she thought.

"How many of you noticed one of them left his banana behind?"

"They had bananas?" asks Justin.

Mr. Hecht picks it up from the desk and dangles it so Justin can see.

"As you can see, this class needs to work on its observational skills," continues Mr. Hecht. "From here on in you pay close attention to what goes on around you. *Close* attention."

Chapter Three

"**W**oodward and Bernstein slay!" shouts Minnie upon entering the classroom.

After a brief pause, Mr. Hecht says, "I have no idea what that means."

"It means they killed it."

Yet another pause. "English, please."

"They're the best."

"You mean 'they're the cat's pajamas!'" Now the pause is from Minnie. "I guess."

The class files in and everyone takes his seat as the late bell rings.

"Minnie's enthusiasm for Woodard and Bernstein can mean only one thing," says Mr. Hecht. "She's finished reading *All the President's Men.*"

He writes, "Bob Woodward" and "Carl Bernstein" on the board.

"These two reporters are the standard we want to live up to. I expect everyone to have finished reading the book by a week from Friday when we will have a quiz." The class moans.

"You heard me. It won't be anything too difficult, just basic information you'll know from reading it. Remember, you're journalists and journalists not only write, they read. Now everyone pour yourself some Joe and we'll get started."

***

School is over for the day and Minnie and Tracy walk through the busy hall.

"So what do you think of Morton Damm?" Tracy inquires. Minnie replies with a noncommittal "Nothing."

"I think he likes you."

"Oh, please! No boys in this school like me and that's fine with me."

Just then they pass Eddie Hanson and a group of boys as he makes armpit noises for their amusement.

"He's not like these idiots," states Tracy.

"You only think that because he's new here. All high school boys are immature," argues Minnie.

"That's just not true. Morton is different and I know he likes you."

"How do you know?"

"I just do."

Minnie and Tracy pass through the front doors of the school to see a line of cars with mothers and fathers waiting to pick up their children. Minnie and Tracy say goodbye and go their separate ways. Minnie gets into her mother's SUV.

"Where's Eddie?" asks Mrs. Mornap.

"Washing his hands, I hope," replies Minnie, much to Mrs. Mornap's confusion.

***

"On the board is a list of possible stories to write for our first issue," states Mr. Hecht. "You'll notice the first one is the pep rally. That one will be the lead of the issue. We'll run the story on page one and then have an additional 'center spread,' which will be mostly photographs.

"That's your newest vocabulary word, 'center spread.' A center spread is a story that runs over the two middle pages of a paper. Write that down."

The class writes that down. "We'll go over each possible story and then you can volunteer for which one you want to write. Plus you can pitch me ones you've come up with and God help you if any of them involves lawn mowing.

"Before anyone volunteers for anything, I've decided to assign the front-page story to Minnie."

This does not sit well with Justin.

"Additionally, I'm assigning Morton as her photographer. The two of you will be working together closely."

This annoys Justin even more but it's just what Morton wants to hear.

"No one take this personally," continues Mr. Hecht. "A newspaper staff is a team. And every team puts its best players in the field or on the court in the position that they play best. Right now these are how I see the positions of this team. That might change, but for now this is how it is.

"I have other pep rally stories for a few of you. Another element of a newspaper is the 'sidebar.' Write that down.

"A 'sidebar' is a separate, shorter piece about the same subject as the lead story. Laura, how do you feel about writing a sidebar on the sports teams that will be represented at the rally?"

"Sure!" Laura is thrilled to be assigned a sidebar.

"This will be mostly statistics. What teams are there, how many players they have, who the coaches are... pretty easy to do."

"Chief...." interrupts Justin. "Do you think I can have a sidebar, too?"

"We could use a short article on the parents who will be there. Some of the mothers of the football players will be there. I think some of them will have the opportunity to speak or at least be introduced. Do you think you can do something with that?"

"I'm all over it!" exclaims Justin with far too much confidence.

"OK, on to the list...." says Mr. Hecht, as he turns to the board.

***

The Mornap family sits at the dinner table.

"How was school today, Minnie?" asks Mrs. Mornap.

Minnie isn't sure what to say. Part of her is thrilled to be assigned the lead story for the first issue, but another part of her wants to be just another kid in the class. She knows if she tells her parents there will be no end to the questions because they'll be so happy.

After a moment of debate she decides to tell them.

"Mr. Hecht assigned me the lead story for the first edition of the paper today." Sure enough, the questions follow.

"Really?!" asks Mrs. Mornap with far too much enthusiasm. "What's the story?"

"The pep rally."

"Sounds exciting! What do you have to do?"

"Who, what, when, where and if I can, how and why."

"I can't wait to go!"

Now she's done it. Her mom wants to go.

"You want to go?!"

"I want to see my baby on her first newspaper assignment."

"You can't! I mean... I'll be busy. I have to work very closely with the photographer."

"Ooo, a photographer? What's her name?"

Minnie mumbles under her breath, "Morton Damm."

"Morgan Vann? I don't know her."

Minnie says his name again, a bit louder. Mrs. Mornap looks over at her husband for help, but he only shrugs.

"Who?"

"Morton Damm! His name is Morton Damm!" confesses Minnie. "He's new."

"OK, OK, no need to yell." Mrs. Mornap gives her husband a secret look of approval.

***

"From here on in, everyone carries one of these!" Mr. Hecht announces as he holds up a memo pad.

"And of course, something to write with. A memo pad costs one federal diploma — also known as a dollar — and everyone here can afford one. You carry it with you wherever you go.

"Another thing each of you should have is a package of colored index cards. Colored index cards are a great way to organize your facts and quotes.

"And if you can afford it, buy one of these...." as he holds up a small digital recorder.

"I don't expect you to run out and buy one, but if you have the money to spare, it's a great investment for a reporter. And Morton, you carry that camera wherever you go.

"The pep rally is tomorrow, fourth period. I happen to know our principal, Mr. McNamara, will begin with an opening speech. I also happen to have that speech right here." He holds up a few type-written pages.

"This is what we call 'advance material.' Write that down. We know he's going to make this speech; we've been given the speech, so that makes it easy for us to incorporate it into our article.

"Sometimes this can backfire. An interesting story about advance material is the famous American poet, Robert Frost, was to recite a poem at President Kennedy's inauguration.

"The newspapers were given the poem as advance material. But when the time came to read it, the sunlight bounced off the page and Frost, being quite old at the time, was blinded by the light and couldn't see the copy. So instead he read a poem he had memorized. The newspapers the next day had the wrong poem in them."

He hands the speech to Minnie. "Here, you'll need this. While the pep rally is our lead story, it's not our only story. Right here, on these index cards, are the remaining possible stories for the first issue. We'll spend the rest of the period assigning stories to those who didn't get one yesterday. As each story is assigned, I'll pin it to the bulletin board with the others. Let's get to work...."

***

Minnie wanders through the pharmacy, searching for the school supplies aisle. She reads the signs hanging from above and finds the one she's looking for. As she continues down the aisle, who should she see but Morton.

"Morton!" she shouts. He turns around and is more than pleased to see her. "I came here for a memo pad."

"So did I," says Morton. "There's one problem, though... they're all pink!"

Minnie takes a look at the selection, and indeed, they're all pink. She has an idea.

"I was thinking about one of those digital recorders. Do you think they sell them here?"

"Let's take a look."

They find the electronics aisle and sure enough, there are two, small digital recorders behind the sliding, glass doors.

***

As Minnie and Morton walk from the cashier towards the exit, Justin comes running in. He stops in his tracks when he sees his two rivals. "Hi, Justin," says Minnie.

Justin isn't in the mood for small talk. He looks at them for a beat and runs away, leaving Minnie and Morton a bit confused.

***

"OK, let's see what you've got," says Mr. Hecht, as he meanders down each row of desks. There's a wide variety of memo pads atop of each. Then he sees Minnie and Morton's recorders. "Nice... very nice, you two." He looks over at Justin.

"Whatchoo hiding there, son?"

Justin reluctantly produces his pink memo pad. The class laughs.

"It's all they had!" Justin explains.

"No need to be ashamed, son. It may be pink, but it'll do the job. OK, back to business. The pep rally is fourth period. You all have your assignments... those who are covering it. The rest of you aren't on vacation. If you see something photo-worthy, take a picture. If you see or hear something of interest, by all means pursue it. If you do, don't forget quotes! First thing tomorrow show me what you've got."

***

Minnie and Morton stand in the corner of the gym. Minnie with her recorder in hand and Morton with his camera around his neck. The entire student body populates the bleachers. Everyone looks bored and a few look like they're about to fall asleep.

"There doesn't seem to be a lot of pep in the room," observes Minnie.

"Maybe things will get more exciting once they start," replies Morton.

Just then the band, which is seated in folding chairs in the corner, strikes up the school's marching song. Or it could be the French national anthem, no one is sure, because no one knows what either song sounds like.

"Shouldn't they be marching?" asks Minnie. "They're a marching band."

"They're not marching," says Morton.

When they're finished playing, there's very little applause.

The varsity cheerleaders take the floor. They perform their cheers with a look of boredom on their faces. No one is buying whatever it is they're selling.

They prance off the floor and the principal, Mr. McNamara, approaches a microphone.

"HELLOOOO SUCCOTASH CENTRAL HIGH SCHOOL!" he bellows.

There is mostly silence. Minnie could swear she hears crickets. He begins to read from the type-written pages. It sounds like he's reading from a poorly-written script.

"I am your principal, Mr. McNamara. Today we kick off another great school year. The first pep rally is one of my favorite days of the year. That and paydays."

Much like Eddie Hanson, he waits for a laugh that doesn't come. Only another cricket.

Minnie gestures to Morton that they should get closer to the principal. They walk several yards in his direction.

"What is pep?" he continues. "The dictionary says pep is 'lively spirits or energy' and 'vigor.' What is a rally? The very same dictionary says it's 'a drawing or coming together of persons for a common cause.'

"So there you have it." He looks up from the pages to see a gymnasium full of students who look bored and couldn't care less about pep or a rally. He continues reading.

"Back in the day when I was a chemistry teacher...." Mr. McNamara gets short of breath. He reaches into his inside, jacket pocket and produces and inhaler. He takes a hit.

For some reason Morton finds this both funny and picture-worthy. In an instant he takes a picture. Even though his flash illuminates the entire room, the principal doesn't notice.

"Pardon me," he continues. "Back in the day when I was a chemistry teacher we had a pep rally that I'll never forget. Why? Because it was the day the bank foreclosed on my house!"

Was this supposed to be another joke? Since no one was listening, it really doesn't matter.

"This is no joke. I've had my share of financial problems in my life which is why I'm pleased to say I'm back here for a new school year. Now let the pep and the rally begin!"

More crickets.

***

The next morning the journalism class sits looking rather confused. Mr. Hecht knows exactly what's going on.

"I know exactly what's going on," he states. "The event wasn't as newsworthy as you'd thought it would be, was it?"

"It was awful!" exclaims Laura. "Everyone was so bored. I overheard two guys arguing over who was going to have a worse season this year, varsity or junior varsity. So I interviewed them and got some quotes, but it's not a flattering story."

"Believe it or not, I'm kind of glad this happened," says Mr. Hecht, to everyone's surprise.

"We in the newspaper business walk a fine line between what the truth is and what we're expected to write. Where do you think the money comes from to publish a newspaper?"

"Subscriptions." says Justin, confidently.

"You would think so," says Mr. Hecht, "but the revenue from subscriptions alone isn't nearly enough to publish a paper." Justin sinks in his chair. "Anyone else have an idea?"

"Advertising?" asks Minnie.

"That's correct," says Mr. Hecht. "Sometimes when the news isn't pretty, and the advertisers aren't going to like to see the truth in the paper, the publisher is in a tough position. Does he run the story as is because it's the truth and run the risk of the advertiser taking his business to another paper, or does he kill the story, or write it in such a way that the advertiser will like, just to keep his business?"

"He has to tell the truth," says one girl. "If it's what happened, he has to tell it that way."

"You would think so," says Mr. Hecht once again. "But the sad truth is we're all dependent upon money and those who are paying the bills — our salaries included — and we're at the mercy of what they want. Now in our case, who is paying for the production of our paper?"

"The taxpayers!" exclaims Justin.

"Uh... ultimately, yes, but our budget comes directly from administration. That would be the principal and the superintendent. They have the authority to put us out of business if they'd like. It's pretty much their newspaper, not ours."

"I wrote up my story last night," says Minnie, "and they're not going to like it. I wrote what I saw. I saw very little pep at a pep rally."

"My best picture is of four kids falling asleep," says Morton. It kind of goes with Minnie's story."

"Photographs don't lie," says Mr. Hecht. "So what do we do? Do we write the stories to keep administration happy or do we write the truth?" asks Mr. Hecht.

The class is quiet. No one wants to be the one to speak first.

"I'll tell you what," says Mr. Hecht. "We'll take a vote. Everyone close his eyes." Everyone does.

"Those who want to tell the truth, raise your hands." All but one raises his hand. "Now those who want to write the stories to keep administration happy, raise your hands." Justin is the only one with his hand up.

Chapter Four

"Coffee! Coffee! Where's the *coffee*?!" shouts Laura and she trembles her way into the classroom.

"Somebody give Laura a fix," says Mr. Hecht. Justin is all over it.

"I've read all your copy," continues Mr. Hecht. "I've got mostly good news. That is all of you have written fine articles for your first attempt. *Almost* all of you." Mr. Hecht glances over at Justin.

"Everyone answered the basic questions needed to create a complete story. *Almost* everyone." He glances over at Justin again.

"We have one student in here who has a natural talent for newspaper work." Mr. Hecht swings his look from Justin to Minnie. Minnie is half thrilled and half embarrassed.

"C'mon, Chief, let's hear who it is!" requests Justin, not knowing he isn't going to like the answer.

"The one with the natural talent is Minnie and the one who didn't quite get it is you."

This comes as no surprise to everyone except Justin. "What's wrong with my article, Chief?!"

"Justin," begins Mr. Hecht, "I asked you to write a sidebar on the parents attending the pep rally. It's mostly 'who' and 'why,' there's really no 'how, what or when,' yet you barely got those two down."

Justin is sorry he asked. "I did a little fact checking," continues Mr. Hecht. "Oh, that's another vocab word you need to know... 'fact checking.' It's exactly what it sounds like. Someone other than the reporter checks the facts in the article before it goes to press. Write that down.

"While the facts you have are 100% accurate, you left out several names. Do you know what that means when the paper comes out? Phone calls! E-mails! Tweets, whatever they are! In short — lots of complaints.

"Part of what this paper does is public relations and the more people we can include the better. Those parents who attended will want to see their names in the paper. I know a sidebar isn't a big deal, but it still has to be good reportage. This is pretty sloppy work."

For some reason Morton decides to come to Justin's rescue by changing the subject. "Uh, Chief, anything about my pictures?"

"Oh, yeah, pictures. They're fine. The one of the four sleeping boys at the pep rally is a hoot. It's going on page one." Morton wasn't expecting *that*. "Along with Minnie's article."

Minnie and Morton give each other a knowing glance. Justin sits there and stews.

"We'll spend the rest of the week laying out the paper together. We'll do that for the first two or three issues. A few of you will be naturals at layout and then I'll turn that over to you for the rest of the year.

"And one last thing. A good reporter knows when to keep his mouth shut. I don't want any of you telling anyone what we're up to. Let them find out when the paper is distributed. Any questions?"

There are no questions. "OK, then, let's get started."

***

Ordinarily a retractable wall divides the gym in two — one side for the boys' P.E. class and one side for the girls'. Today the wall has been retracted — hence its name —and both classes occupy the gym, although the boys stay on their side and the girls on the other.

Minnie and Tracy have P.E. the same period. Up until this point they didn't know Morton has it, too, but now they do because they can see him across the gym. Each student is in his or her gym uniform — a white t-shirt with green trim and matching green shorts.

"I swear Morton Damm likes you, you know," says Tracy.

"So you keep telling me," replies Minnie. "But how do you know?"

"He's looking at you right now," says Tracy. They slowly turn their heads towards the boys' side of the gym and sure enough, Morton is looking in their direction. When he sees them looking at him, he gives a big wave.

"Told you so," says Tracy.

"It's no big deal. Except that...."

"Except what?!" demands Tracy.

"Except that I kind of like him, too," confesses Minnie.

"I knew it! I *knew* it!" exclaims Tracy. She knows this changes things. "I guess this will be the end of me... at least for a while."

***

"Staff..." begins Mr. Hecht, "...we have a newspaper!" The class cheers.

"I put the finishing touches on the layout after school yesterday, put it to bed and sent the thing to the printer. Here's what happens next: it will take a few days for it to be printed and delivered here. When it is we'll each distribute it to the homerooms first period and then come back here to have a little party.

"And by that I mean a breakfast party. I'll stop by the diner on my way in and pick up eggs and home fries and such. As usual, you bring your own coffee."

This reminds Mr. Hecht of something. "Justin, how's that contraption working?"

"We're a little low on supplies, Chief," says Justin.

"Do you think you can get restocked in the next day or two?" asks Mr. Hecht.

"Sure thing, Chief. No need to bring coffee for the party, I'll have it for everyone."

"Jim Dandy!" says Mr. Hecht. "Bring me receipts. Now for the bad news: while we're waiting for the paper to be printed it's quiz time. You have today and tomorrow to study up on the new vocab words plus *All the President's Men*. If you haven't finished reading it yet, now's the time.

"They'll be basic question you'll know from reading it, nothing too detailed. You can spend the rest of the period reading or studying your vocabulary words. If you're up to speed on everything then I have a few copies of today's *New York Times* on hand."

Chapter Five

"'Too Pooped to Pep,' Mr. Hecht?" says Mr. McNamara, as he stares down his new enemy, who's seated across his desk.

That very headline is atop the front page of the paper which lies lifeless between them. "What were you thinking?"

"We had a rather lively discussion about this in class and the students wanted to publish the truth. We took a vote," explains Mr. Hecht, although he knows it will do no good.

"A vote? A *vote*! A classroom is not a democracy. *You* make the decisions and the decisions *you* make are the ones *I want*!

This is the fifth principal at the school Mr. Hecht has worked for. They don't seem to last long. Every few years there's someone new. He doesn't know where they come from or where they go to but they come and go.

McNamara has been there for three years and this is the first time Mr. Hecht has been called into his office.

"OK. Sure. Fine."

"Now that's more like it. I expect to see happy, inoffensive articles in the next paper."

***

The bell rings at the end of first period. As the class files out of the room, Minnie approaches Mr. Hecht.

"Chief," she begins. "I have good news and I have bad news. The good news is my parents are very happy with how you teach this class and all the help you've been giving me. The bad news is they want to take you out to dinner."

"Dinner, huh?" replies Mr. Hecht. "I can think of worse things. It's not going to be sushi, is it?"

"Oh, no," laughs Minnie. "They're more the steakhouse type."

"OK, then steak it is."

"Can you meet us at Tommy's Steakhouse at six o'clock on Friday?"

"It's a date," says Mr. Hecht. "I mean... I'll be there."

***

Mr. Hecht walks into Tommy's Steakhouse with reluctance. When he was a beat reporter he had no problem walking up to a complete stranger who had just witnessed a murder and start asking him questions.

But talking to people he knows at events such as dinner parties and wedding receptions are, at times, torture to him.

Tonight shouldn't be too bad, he thinks. If Minnie's parents are anything like Minnie, how bad could it be?

He sees the Mornap family at a table across the room. He makes his way over and naturally this is that awkward time for introductions. Minnie is no dope, though, and makes them quick and painless.

Mr. Hecht takes his seat. "Do we call you Chief, too?" asks Mrs. Mornap. Mr. Hecht laughs. "Ben is fine."

Just as everyone gets settled, Mrs. Mornap's phone rings. She and her husband look at each other with a trace of panic on their faces. Clearly, they were expecting this call at some point.

Mrs. Mornap looks at the caller ID and stands up.

"Excuse me, please."

As she hurries away from the table, Mr. Mornap stands and says, "Me, too."

Minnie knows Mr. Hecht has no idea what's going on, so she offers an explanation.

"My mother and my aunts were always close. When my grandmother died, she had my mother promise her she'd look after her younger sisters, since she's the oldest. Well, my aunts are always having problems.

"One is a missionary in Africa and she's in bad health. We knew the phone call was going to come soon, but this is sooner than we thought.

"My parents have been packed for days, ready to leave when they have to."

"It looks like they have to," says Mr. Hecht.

Mr. Mornap returns to the table.

"Ben, I'm sorry but we have to go," he says. He removes his wallet and hands Minnie a credit card. "Pay for dinner with this."

He's gone in a flash.

"They're going to leave you home alone?" asks Mr. Hecht.

"It's not the first time," replies Minnie. "The lady next door comes over and checks in on me. They know I'm not going to have any wild parties!"

"We *all* know that," says Mr. Hecht, which gets a smile out of Minnie.

Chapter Six

"Not every article in a newspaper is actually news," begins Mr. Hecht. "Can anyone name a type of article that's in a paper every day but not news?"

Mr. Hecht looks over the class. He can smell the wood burning. Justin is dying to answer at least one question correctly but nothing is coming to him. Nothing is coming to anyone until Minnie's hand slowly rises.

"Minnie!"

"A review?"

"Absolutely!" says Mr. Hecht, who knew Minnie would get it right. "A movie review, a restaurant review, a concert review... not really news but an integral part of a newspaper. Here's another and one of my favorite kinds of articles...."

Mr. Hecht turns to the board and writes, "Profile Pieces."

"A profile piece is an article usually about an individual but can be about a pair or a group that works together and there's something about him (or them) that makes him noteworthy.

"For example, say you know someone who was born with a condition that makes his life very difficulty physically. He's in a wheelchair and can barely write his own name. But he doesn't let this stop him from succeeding... he becomes an honor student and then gets accepted to Yale!

"An article about this person, along with a picture, would make a nice profile piece because his story is interesting enough for us to want to know it.

"Here's your assignment: find someone worthy of a profile piece. It doesn't matter who it is... an administrator, a teacher, a lunch lady, a groundskeeper... anyone with a story worth telling. Keep in mind any story about overcoming obstacles generally makes a good profile piece. If everybody writes one, we can run at least one in each issue until the year is out."

***

Minnie and Morton meander through the hallway, eyes pealed looking for someone worthy of a profile piece. The other students zip by them, all in a hurry.

"Mr. Hecht said it can be about anyone," repeats Minnie. "I don't see any possibilities right now."

"He said it can be about a teacher... but most of my teachers are kind of dull," laments Morton. "My photography teacher is kind of goofy, though."

"Goofy is nice, but that's not going to make a great article. I need someone with a real story to tell," says Minnie.

Her gaze falls upon a Hispanic custodian, cleaning the windows in a pair of fire doors with a spray bottle and paper towels. She stops walking, leaving plenty of distance between him and them.

"What do you think his story is?" she asks Morton. "Immigrants often have a story, don't they?"

"I guess," says Morton. "Want to ask him?"

"I think I do," says Minnie decisively. "Wait here."

She steps away from Morton, whose eyes follow her as she marches up to the custodian.

Boy, he really likes this girl.

***

Minnie sits in the custodians' office. You can hardly call it an office, although it has a desk with a phone, so Minnie deduces those are the two things that make an office an office, therefore it must be an office.

Seated at the desk is the custodian she saw in the hallway. Minnie sits opposite him, with her recorder atop the desk. She has a list of questions prepared on one of her father's legal pads.

"Let's start with the basics. What's your name and where are you from?" begins Minnie.

"My name is Manuel Montoya and I am of Ecuador," answers Manuel.

"Ecuador is a long way from here. How did you get here?" asks Minnie, with true interest in knowing the answer.

"Many people in South America live in poverty. We hear that America is the Land of Opportunity and we want to come here to make a better life for our families. But there are many obstacles."

Minnie loves the word "obstacles."

"There are two ways to move to America: The legal way and the illegal way. I could not chance the safety of my family coming here illegally, so I had to do many, many things that were required to move us here legally. I don't do illegal things, anyway."

"Before you tell me how you did that, I have to say your English is excellent. How did you learn English?" interrupts Minnie.

"First I listened to American music. But they sing very fast! A friend knew some English and he taught me what he knew, but it wasn't enough. When I arrived here I could barely speak. But then I found a free class to learn at night. I went for months. It worked!"

The more Manuel says the more intrigued Minnie becomes.

Minnie asks herself, "Do any of the hundreds of students who pass Manuel in the hallway each day have any idea of his story?"

"Probably not," she deduces. "I certainly didn't."

"Many people in my country live in fear. Sometimes there are officials who are corrupt. If the police arrive at your door, there's a good chance you will be put in prison with no trial," continues Manuel.

Manuel tells Minnie his whole story. How after arriving in the US, he had to take odd jobs mowing lawns and cleaning gutters to make a few dollars to feed his wife and son. How out of desperation he turned to a charity for help, even though he was humiliated to ask.

But then the miracle happened and he was hired as a custodian at Succotash Central High School and he has a regular income and health benefits for his family and he no longer has to depend on charities.

"Do you have a picture of your family?" asks Minnie.

Manuel stands up. "Come with me."

He walks her over to a short row of lockers, one for each custodian in the building. Manuel's has a big "M.M." on it.

"I see we have the same initials," says Minnie.

Manuel opens the door, which was not locked, and shows her photographs taped to the inside. They're all of him, his wife and his son.

The interview lasted well over an hour and even then, Minnie wanted to hear more. When she stood up to leave, she couldn't help but think what a wonderful profile piece this will make.

***

Morton sits impatiently on the low, brick wall that is the perimeter of the school. He looks at his watch — again — even though he looked at it seconds before. He gets up and starts to pace.

Finally, the wait is over. Minnie comes running up, almost skipping, twirling her digital recorder on her finger by the strap.

"I have a great interview! It should make a wonderful profile piece. I'm so happy!"

Not quite realizing what she's doing, she gives Morton a huge hug. Naturally, he hugs her back.

They look at each other, face-to-face for a moment, and both come to the conclusion that this is more than a celebratory hug... this is the real thing.

Without thinking about it, Minnie kisses Morton right on the lips, open mouth, the real deal.

They stop for a moment, look in each others eyes and kiss again, this time with passion and emotion neither knew he or she had. There's not a sliver of light between them.

Minnie had a million thoughts at once. The biggest one was, "How do I know how to do this? This is my first kiss yet I seem to know how to do it. I guess that's what they call, 'Doing what comes naturally.'"

It was not only natural, it was logical, just the way Minnie likes it.

***

"You *what*?!" shouts Tracy.

"I... kissed Morton Damm. You heard me the first time."

"I knew it! I *knew* it!"

"Stop saying that!" says Minnie. "It's no big deal."

"No big deal?! Let me ask you this: who kissed who?"

Minnie knows Tracy isn't going to like the answer but she cannot tell a lie.

"I kissed him first. But then he kissed me back! And then we kissed each other."

"I *knew* it!" repeats Tracy.

"Stop saying that!"

"So what happens next?" inquires Tracy.

"I don't know. I've never had a boyfriend before. And neither have you. So when I find out I'll tell you."

Chapter Seven

Mr. Hecht learned many things during his time as a beat reporter but the single most important one was to be early. Not just on time, but early. Being the first person at an event presented far more opportunities than being just one of the crowd.

So as usual, Mr. Hecht arrives at school long before he has to. Today, however, is a bit different. Upon arrival the parking lot is a beehive of activity, with police cars, fire trucks and even the bomb squad.

The bomb squad? What's this all about? Mr. Hecht parks his car and sets out on foot to get a closer look. To his surprise, Minnie is already at school.

"Minnie?"

"Oh, hi Chief."

"What's this all about?"

"It seems there was an explosion. Look at the building."

A wing of the building is in bad shape. Basement windows blown out and soot on the exterior walls.

"Tracy's father has a police scanner — which is no surprise — so he wanted to be the first lawyer here. Tracy called and we came right over."

The relatively calm atmosphere of the location is shattered when a police dog is walked out of the building followed by two officers escorting an individual.

It's difficult to see just who it is with the commotion of the reporters and camerapeople each vying for a position.

The commotion crescendos when the individual runs. Minnie gets a good look at who it is.

"Manuel!" she cries.

One of the police officers chases after him. Manuel doesn't get but a few yards when he's tackled to the ground and handcuffed.

***

"There is absolutely nothing wrong," states the principal as he tries to maintain his best poker face. "Everything is fine."

Minnie can't believe what she's hearing, as she sits in the same "hot seat" Mr. Hecht was in a short time before. Instead of the school year's first issue of the newspaper atop the desk between them, it's Minnie's recorder that sets there.

"There was an explosion at the school yesterday; how can you say there's nothing wrong?" demands Minnie.

"It was an accident. Accidents happen. It was either a gas leak or fumes from one of the cleaners the custodians use was ignited by a cigarette or something. Those guys are just the type to be smoking on school property.

"The fire marshal is looking into it and I'm sure the answer will be something simple."

"Then why did the police arrest Manuel?"

"That was their idea. I had nothing to do with that. They wanted to take him in for questioning and he ran. The dog found something and they did what they had to do."

"Why was the bomb squad here and a K-9 unit?"

Mr. McNamara starts to get fidgety.

"I suppose the fire chief overacted a little. Those guys are under a lot of pressure."

He starts to get short of breath. He pats his jacket pocket and when he doesn't feel anything inside, he checks the side pockets. When there's nothing in those, he opens the drawers in his desk, two at a time.

"I need my inhaler but it's not here. Now where can it be?" He thinks for a moment. "I'm sure it will turn up."

"Are there any charges against Manuel?" asks Minnie.

"I can't comment on an on-going police investigation. All I can tell you is not to worry; the school will be back to normal in no time."

The look of disbelief on Minnie's face intensifies. This guy has told her nothing useful for an article.

"Clearly I need to talk to someone else," deduces Minnie.

***

Manuel and Mr. Mornap sit opposite each other at a large table in the conference room of

Mornap & Turner. Neither says a word to the other. Clearly they are waiting for something.

Minnie comes running into the room. She's what they're waiting for. Minnie takes a seat next to her father.

"Manuel," begins Mr. Mornap as he opens a file folder. "The charges against you are very severe. The first one is you were running a meth lab out of a room in the school basement and the second one is the room blew up. If found guilty of these charges, you will go to prison for many years.

"Do you know what a meth lab is?"

Manuel shakes his head almost imperceptibly.

"Meth is short for methamphetamine," says Mr. Mornap. "It's an illegal drug and very addictive. It's also very lucrative. Meth suppliers and dealers make a lot of money from addicts."

"I have never heard of meth," whispers Manuel.

"It's made by mixing, heating and crystalizing various chemicals in a lab using burners and containers that can withstand the heat. And that's exactly what the police found in the basement of the school."

Mr. Mornap produces several photographs from the file folder; all of them are of what's left of the apparatus from the meth lab. Manuel glances at them.

"I have never been in that room," whispers Manuel. "I do not know what these things are called. I've seen them in the chemistry classroom but that's it."

The word "chemistry" strikes a chord with Minnie. "But why?" she asks herself.

"If you're innocent, why did you run?" asks Mr. Mornap.

"Scared," is Manuel's one-word answer.

"The police dog found traces of meth on a handkerchief in your locker. Do you have any idea how it got on there?"

Once again, Manuel shakes his head. "That's not my handkerchief," states Manuel.

Minnie and Mr. Mornap look at each other. Minnie knows right then and there that Manuel was set up. She knew that already but this just confirmed it. She also knows if he's going to be exonerated, he's going to need her help.

***

Minnie sits in English class. They're reading *Hamlet*. Well, the rest of the class is reading *Hamlet*. All Minnie can think about is Manuel.

The teacher, Mr. Messenger, presses on.

"'Now might I do it pat. Now he is praying,' says Hamlet. What he's talking about is killing King Claudius right then and there but he doesn't do it. Why?"

Mr. Messenger looks around the room. He sees Minnie has completely checked out.

"Minnie... why doesn't Hamlet kill him now and avenge his father's murder?"

There's no answer from Minnie. The whole class looks at her and she has no idea she's the center of attention.

"Minnie...?" says Mr. Messenger.

Minnie snaps out of her trance... sort of.

"He's got something to hide," says Minnie.

"We know the king has something to hide; he killed Hamlet's father. But that's not why Hamlet doesn't kill him now. Why doesn't he?"

"There are too many unanswered questions," states Minnie.

Mr. Messenger is a bit confused. "What do you mean?"

"The handkerchief. How did the meth get on the handkerchief?"

"First off, I don't think there's a handkerchief in *Hamlet* and secondly I'm positive there's no meth in the play, either. What are you talking about?"

"If I can figure out *how* he was set up then I'll know *why*," says Minnie.

"I can't argue with that logic," says Mr. Messenger.

"Uh... I have to step out for a minute. Girl problems."

That's the last thing Mr. Messenger wants to hear.

"Fill out a pass," is all he says.

Minnie learned in seventh grade the two words that can get her out of an awkward situation are "girl problems." However, they only work with male teachers and her father. Female teachers and her mother know too much.

***

It's after school. Minnie and Morton sit in the bleachers on the edge of the football field.

The marching band rehearses in front of them and the color guard practices off in the distance.

"Let's look at the facts," says Minnie. "Someone was running a meth lab in the school basement. But who?"

"I guess someone who had access to the school basement," says Morton.

"Who would that be?" asks Minnie.

"Almost anyone. I never counted them but there must be four or five custodians, then the guys who fix things...."

Morton's gaze wanders to the edge of the football field. He sees someone riding a lawnmower.

"And then there are the lawnmower guys," he says.

"They're called 'groundskeepers,'" says Minnie.

"Whatever they're called there must be a few of them and they all work out of the basement."

"Morton has a point," thinks Minnie. "Then I need to narrow it down somehow," she says out loud.

"I know you'll find just the way to do that," says Morton with a smile and a look of pride as he stares into Minnie's eyes.

He leans in and softly kisses her lips. She really doesn't kiss him back. All she can think about is what to do next.

***

It's an hour before the start of school and Minnie stands in front of the building. A half-asleep Morton staggers up to her.

"OK, I'm here. But I don't know why," he mumbles. "I brought my camera as you told me to."

"Come with me."

"Where?"

"To the crime scene. To find clues."

"'To find clues'?! I think you're taking this investigative reporting a little too far."

"If you're planning on kissing these lips again you'll help me find clues."

"Let's go find some clues!"

***

Minnie and Morton make their way down the stairs to the part of the basement that had the explosion. It's no longer a crime scene because the detectives are finished looking for their own clues. But the place is still roped off with yellow tape.

"What do you expect to find?" asks Morton.

"I'm not sure. Maybe nothing. But I have to look."

They stand at the edge of the crime scene tape. Morton is too scared to touch it. Minnie rolls her eyes and lifts it so they can both pass underneath.

"Get a few pictures of the place," instructs Minnie. Morton takes a few shots of the hallway.

They peek into the room that housed the meth lab. It's a wreck. All the items that concocted the actual drug have been taken by the police. All that remains are the charred walls, broken windows and what's left of the tables.

"Hmm... there's nothing left in here," laments Minnie. "Let's just think for a minute. I'm sure that handkerchief was planted in Manuel's locker. So the guilty party needed to go into the custodian's office — over here," as she walks toward the office, "— leave the handkerchief and then get out."

"The only way out is up those stairs," says Morton.

"Then let's go up those stairs."

They walk up the first part of the stairs to the landing where there's a garbage can recessed into the wall. Minnie pauses and gives it a look.

"I wonder if the police looked in here," she ponders.

"I know *you're* going to," says Morton.

Minnie gives the front a yank, which opens the unit from the top with the hinge on the bottom. She looks inside.

"Don't touch anything," she says. She reaches into her bag and produces a rubber glove — the kind you wash dishes with — and a zip-lock bag.

"How did you know to bring those?" asks Moron.

"I just knew," says Minnie. Morton feels her intelligence makes her even more attractive.

She puts the glove on one hand and holds the open bag with the other.

She reaches into the garbage can and pulls out what looks like an inhaler broken into several pieces. Minnie and Morton look at each other for a moment and she places the pieces into the bag.

***

It's lunchtime. The cafeteria is abuzz with hungry teenagers. Those poor lunch ladies.

Morton stands on the chow line. Minnie rushes up to him.

"Let's go!"

"Where are we going now?

"To a drug store. To talk to a pharmacist. I've been thinking about this all morning."

"Do we have to?"

Minnie points to her lips.

"I'll drive!"

"You don't have a license."

"Oh, right. Then we'll walk."

***

Minnie and Morton pass through the front doors of the school and continue walking at a brisk pace.

"We'll be late for sixth period," bemoans Morton.

"The pharmacy is two blocks away and if we're late getting back, I'll have the Chief write us a pass."

"This girl is pretty smart," thinks Morton. "Pretty *and* smart, that is. Maybe I better keep my mouth shut and do whatever she wants. Yes, that's a good idea," he concludes.

***

Minnie and Morton stand face-to-face with the pharmacist, although a counter separates him from them. He's quite a bit older and originally from Korea. Clearly he's been in America for a long time judging from his perfect English and barely traceable accent.

"What can I do for you, young lady?" asks the pharmacist.

"I'm writing... a story... for school... and I want to make sure I have all my facts straight," says Minnie. While it's the truth, it's only half the truth.

"A short story?" asks the pharmacist?

"Something like that," lies Minnie. "An inhaler for asthma, what's inside of one of them?"

"There are many kinds of inhalers, each with different contents," replies the pharmacist. Do you have one in particular in mind?"

Minnie hesitates for a moment, not sure if showing him the inhaler she found is a good idea or not. After a beat she deduces she must show it to him if she wants an accurate answer.

She reaches into her bag and hands the inhaler to him, still in the zip-lock bag. He looks it over.

"What do you want to know, specifically?" he asks.

"Well, the 'character' in my story gets framed for a crime he didn't commit because a police dog finds traces of meth on him and I want to make it that the real culprit cracked this open and planted whatever's inside on him. And then a police dog finds it, thinking it's meth," says Minnie, hoping the pharmacist doesn't catch on.

"That's quite a story," laughs the pharmacist.

"Is it plausible?" asks Minnie. "I want to be 100 percent accurate... for my story."

"It's very plausible," replies the pharmacist. "The chemical, mephentermine, is a methadrine-based stimulant. They're in the same family."

"Would you say they're brothers?"

"Half brothers."

"Thank you so much," says Minnie, as she takes the inhaler back.

Minnie and Morton turn and take a step towards the door when Minnie is overcome with guilt. She stops and turns around. Morton follows her lead.

"There's something I should tell you," confesses Minnie. "This isn't for a short story but for a newspaper article. But it *is* for school — for the school newspaper."

"I figured that out already," says the pharmacist. "It's about that explosion."

Minnie doesn't know whether to be relieved or worried.

"May I quote you in the article?" asks Minnie.

"Just make sure you spell my name right," says the pharmacist. "Here," as he hands her a business card.

Chapter Eight

"Jumpin Johosephat!" exclaims Mr. Hecht. "You think the principal was running a methamphetamine lab out of the school, blew it up and set the janitor up to take the fall?!"

"I can prove it," says Minnie without emotion.

"Show me what you've got."

Minnie and Morton cross to a table. Mr. Hecht follows right behind. Minnie removes colored index cards from her bag as well as any evidence she's collected and Morton's photographs. As she lays each item on the table, she explains how it's an integral piece of the puzzle.

"We know these facts about the principal: he was a chemistry teacher and he's had money problems. We know these facts because they're in his pep rally speech. This speech," as she lays the speech on the table.

"We also know he uses an inhaler for his asthma. Here's a photograph of him using it," she says as she places Morton's handy work next to the advance material.

"I found this in a garbage can near the crime scene," she says as she lays the broken inhaler in the zip-lock bag next on the table.

"I interviewed a pharmacist who says the inside of an inhaler has a stimulant, mephentermine, that's in the same family as meth. Open it up and you have what appears to be an illegal drug you can plant on someone else."

"Did the pharmacist say this on the record?" asks Mr. Hecht.

"He said I can quote him," replies Minnie. "And I did."

"Continue," says Mr. Hecht.

Minnie produces an index card that reads, "Manuel's locker."

"Manuel kept his locker unlocked. I noticed that when I interviewed him for my profile piece. I didn't think much of it at the time but when I had to figure out how the handkerchief with the mephentermine was planted, I remembered."

Mr. Hecht sees exactly where this is going. Within the next 30 seconds Minnie will have this case wrapped up.

Minnie produces a newspaper clipping from *The Succotash Sentinel*.

"The newspaper has a photograph of an officer with a dog — the K-9 unit. This is the dog that found the handkerchief in Manuel's locker.

"The police chief is quoted in the article saying when the principal called 911 after the explosion, he requested a K-9 unit. That seems like an odd thing to think of in the middle of a crisis. I mean, your building just blew up and this is what you ask for? Sounds like he wanted the dog to find something."

"The 911 call came at 6:27 am. It's in the article. But the clock on the wall in the hallway outside the room is stopped at 6:18." She produces another of Morton's pictures.

"So what went on for nine minutes? The principal had to come up with a plan — and fast — and then do it. Nine minutes is plenty of time to come up with the plan, crack open the inhaler, plant the evidence, ditch the inhaler in the trash and then call 911."

She produces the last index card that reads, "No inhaler at interview."

"When I interviewed the principal the day after the explosion, he needed his inhaler but didn't have it. I have a recording of him saying it.

"The meth lab was his," states Minnie.

The last item she produces is her article. "Here's my copy."

Mr. Hecht pauses to take all this in. He surveys the items on the table once more looking for a hole in Minnie's argument.

There's no hole.

"You have all of this on a disc?" asks Mr. Hecht.

"Right here," replies Minnie. She hands him a disc.

"I'm going to hold on to both the hardcopies and the disc. You have them saved somewhere else, too, correct?"

"What do you think?"

Mr. Hecht grins at such a stupid question he just asked.

"I have to decide what to do. This is too big for us. I guess the only option is to hand this story over to the city desk at *The Succotash Sentinel*. I have a contact there. But I have to think about this for a while."

***

The train doors open at Grand Central Station in New York City and Mr. Hecht steps on to the platform along with hundreds of faceless strangers, each with a place to go.

Grand Central is only one leg of the trip. Mr. Hecht had to drive a great distance from Succotash Valley in northern New York state just to get to the end (or the beginning) of the train line that would take him into Grand Central. Then from Grand Central he has to take the subway to the Chelsea area of New York City.

It's been a long time since he'd been there, but Mr. Hecht knows the building right away. It looks like all the other apartment buildings in the neighborhood but he has been there so many times before he could never forget it.

Without even thinking about it, he finds the apartment on the fifth floor. With a bit of hesitation he knocks on the door.

"Friend or foe?" asks the old, raspy voice from inside.

"Friend. An old friend," replies Mr. Hecht.

"What's the password?"

A smile comes across Mr. Hecht's face. "Never pay for a story."

He hears the three locks on the door slowly being unbolted, unlatched and unturned. The door opens slowly to reveal someone close to twice Mr. Hecht's age and judging from his weathered face, with twice the experience in the newspaper game.

***

Mr. Hecht sits in the living room. Since it's a studio apartment, the entire place is a living room. He looks at the walls which are covered with framed newspaper pages — yellowed but still legible — and countless awards and black and white photographs, usually with an inscription scrawled on them.

The names and faces in these pictures are ancient history to his students, and in some cases, to Mr. Hecht as well. The "curator" of this "museum" was a newspaper veteran long before Mr. Hecht met him ages ago and many of these mementos were accumulated then.

But the best item hangs solitary on a wall, encased in glass. It's a Pulitzer Prize, the highest award for journalism.

This unassuming apartment with relics from a bygone era is inhabited by Walter Burns. Walter spent his entire career in New York City's newspaper trade, working his way up from the bottom as a copy boy to the managing editor of *The New York Gazette*, which was the most popular tabloid of its day.

The Gazette is long since defunct and the day it folded was the day Walter retired. He enters the living room holding two glasses of beer.

"I only have Pabst," he says to Mr. Hecht, as he hands him one of the glasses.

"That's all you ever drank. They still make this stuff or is this from 50 years ago?"

"Taste it and see."

Mr. Hecht takes a sip. "Tastes like 50."

"Sixty," says Walter, as he takes a seat in the big armchair. "I know this isn't a social visit. It never is with you. What's on your mind?"

"I've got this student — a girl — and she's a natural. I explain a concept and not only does she understand it, she goes out and does it. Her copy is exceptional. And she has that one thing that makes a reporter great: attention to detail. She's good. Really good."

"So this is a problem?" asks Walter.

"The problem is she did a little digging around the school after there was this explosion. Just read the story and you'll know why I'm here."

Mr. Hecht opens his briefcase and hands Walter Minnie's article.

***

"I see what you mean. It appears very thorough."

"It all checks out, as far as I can see. So what do I do?"

"I think you know the answer to that. You're a newspaper man."

"That's just it," agues Mr. Hecht. "They're not paying me to be a newspaper man. They're paying me to be a high school teacher. High school teachers don't crucify their principals. Or do they?"

"Who are you worried about being crucified? Your principal or you?"

"I think *you* know the answer to *that*."

"You know I hated to see you leave the business. This girl is a natural? *You* were the natural. But I know it's no life — look how I wound up. But I also know you have journalism in your blood and you can't change that."

Walter tosses the article onto the coffee table. "Do the right thing."

***

The sun has barely reached above the horizon and Mr. Hecht is up and dressed. He walks out to his front lawn just as a car whizzes by and the driver tosses the morning's newspaper at his feet without slowing down.

Mr. Hecht picks up the paper, removes it from its plastic bag and unfolds it. The front page is a huge picture of McNamara with his lips around his inhaler at the pep rally, taken by Morton.

The headline reads, *Suck on This* with a dek that reads, *Evidence Indicates HS Principal Ran Meth Lab in Basement*. The byline reads, *By Minnie Mornap*.

"These two are good," thinks Mr. Hecht. "These two are very good."

***

Mr. Hecht makes his way to his classroom. As he brings the key toward the lock, he notices the door is ajar. This can't be good.

He slowly pushes the door open to find the district superintendent, Dr. Deirdre Hayes, seated at his desk.

"Mr. Hecht, we have a problem," she dryly states.

"I'll say. The principal you hired is a deadbeat who ran a meth lab out of the school, blew it up and tried to hang it on someone innocent."

"Oh, that. That will blow over. We have a much bigger problem."

"What could be bigger than that?"

"You were seen the other night fraternizing with a student — a female student."

"I don't know what you're talking about."

"Were you not out for dinner at a restaurant with Minnie Mornap?"

"Well, yes, but her parents were there. It was their idea."

"No one saw her parents there. They just saw the both of you. It looked like a date."

"Her parents had to leave in a hurry. I'm sure if you ask them they'll explain everything."

"We've tried calling them. There's no reply."

"That's because they're in Africa. As soon as they get back they can explain everything."

"We're not waiting for that."

"Have you asked Minnie?"

"I'm not asking Minnie anything. She's not trustworthy."

"Not trustworthy?!" exclaims Mr. Hecht. "She's the most trustworthy student I've ever had!"

"Naturally you'd think that. Mr. Hecht, you're fired. You can clean out your room now, hand in your key and then go to the district office to make sure your pension papers are in order."

"I'm twice you're age and twice as smart as you. I know you're firing me because you made a colossal mistake in hiring that crackpot and when one of my students —who's smarter than you'll ever be — figures out what he did, you're too embarrassed for yourself and the crackpot, doc-*tor*."

"Start packing, Mr. Hecht."

***

Minnie couldn't get to school fast enough. The entire trip in Eddie Hanson's mother's car she read and reread the article as it appeared in the paper. Reading in a moving car made her nauseated but she didn't care.

Even though she knew the day before her article was going to be published, seeing it in print — on the front page no less — was just too good to be true.

Too bad her parents weren't there to see it. She had a short conversation with her mother when her parents were in a civilized part of whatever country they were in, right before they left for whatever village her aunt was in.

So she was able to tell them Mr. Hecht wanted to submit the story to the paper and Mrs. Mornap gave him her blessing to do so.

Regardless of her absent parents, surely the *entire school* would be just as happy. This is the big time she deduces, so why *wouldn't* they be happy for her?

As Minnie exits Eddie Hanson's mother's car, she looks around, half expecting a mob to greet her.

There's no mob.

She walks down the hallway. Surely someone will comment to her that he saw the article... or at least heard about it.

No one comments.

The journalism class will *have to* be thrilled, she deduces. They'll just *have to*. As Minnie enters the room, all thoughts of herself and her impending glory disperse like a spurt of perfume from an atomizer.

Something is wrong. Very wrong. Mr. Hecht isn't in the room, but a substitute teacher is. And Dr. Hayes.

The late bell echoes throughout the building. Minnie slowly takes her seat next to Morton. Justin won't even look at her, but that's not really the problem.

The problem is Mr. Hecht isn't there and having the superintendent in the room, along with a sub, is a bad sign. Two bad signs.

"Class," Dr. Hayes begins, "Mr. Hecht is no longer at the school."

The class gasps. What is she talking about?

"He decided he no longer wants to work here and quit this morning. You'll have a sub for a few days while we figure out how to get out of this mess he left us in."

And that's all she says.

***

Mr. Hecht plops himself down at his kitchen table. The morning is only three hours old yet it feels like a week. He picks up the remote and turns on the TV, which is set to the local news station.

There's a breaking news story. McNamara is being arrested at the high school.

It was clockwork:

- The paper runs the story in the early morning edition.
- The district administration panics and fires Mr. Hecht.
- The police go over the details right away.
- It all adds up so they arrest McNamara.

Once again, The Power of the Press cannot be denied.

Chapter Nine

Mr. Hecht sits opposite the secretary of the managing editor of *The Succotash Sentinel*. It's been a long time since he's been at an actual newspaper, and while he feels at home there, something isn't quite right.

It takes him a minute to figure out what it is. There's no clamor of typewriters. In his day, the entire building would have been filled with the cacophony of typewriter keys slapping against paper, creating copy that would be in the next edition. That beautiful noise is long gone and Mr. Hecht will just have to get used to it.

Mr. Hecht isn't sure what to expect. All he knows is they called him. It's always better when they call you.

"Mr. MacArthur will see you now," says the secretary, prompting Mr. Hecht to take that giant step into the boss' office.

Inside the office, Mr. MacArthur warmly greets Mr. Hecht. "Mr. Hecht, I'm Charlie MacArthur. Please have a seat."

"I'll have a seat but please call me Ben. I could never get used to Mr. Hecht."

"I know," says Charlie. "That's why you had your students call you Chief."

"You've done your homework," says Mr. Hecht. "I'm impressed."

"I've got a newspaper to run so I'll get right to the point. I want to hire you. I want you to start a program for teens and you'll pretty much do whatever you did at the high school. Teach them how to put together a story, with photos, and you'll have four pages in the paper whenever you're ready.

"All I want is definitely once a week and if some weeks you have a lot of copy it can be two or three times. The four pages are pretty much yours; I'll trust you'll do the right thing with them."

"That's a very nice offer," replies Mr. Hecht. "But I'll need few things, first."

"Shoot."

"For one, I don't work out of a cubical. I get my own office. Next, I want the section to be part of the Sunday paper and I don't answer to anyone but you. I'll need a second room that's set up like a classroom. It's what I'm used to. And money. I want lots of money."

"We're both newspaper veterans and your preference to be called Chief wasn't the only thing I found out about you," retorts Charlie.

"Most of what I know is a matter of public record. You worked for the public school system so your salary and other figures are public. I see you were at the high end of the pay scale, since you were in the district for so long, and I see you could have retired years ago. I also know what your pension is going to be.

"I just didn't depend on public records; I did a little digging, too. It appears you never got married — and I know marriage and newspaper work don't go together — just ask either of my ex-wives — and since you purchased your house over 20 years ago, it's safe to assume it's paid for. With no kids to send to college, you're doing quite well financially. I certainly *have* done my homework."

"Just because I don't need the money that doesn't mean you can underpay me," says Mr. Hecht.

"I don't intend to underpay you. My offer is the job as I described it; the extras you just stated, compensation will be 70% of your current annual salary; plus full health benefits, two weeks paid vacation and a moderate expense account."

"Who takes care of recruitment or admissions or whatever you want to call it?"

"We'll put the word out but you're more than welcome to invite anyone you think may be a good match. I'll leave the application process and requirements up to you."

"That's very fair. More than fair. I can't turn down an offer like that. There's one more thing, though. You have to hire Minnie and Morton. Put them on the payroll as stringers or contributing writers or whatever you want to call them. These kids have a nose for news it's only going to work if they're part of my team and I want them to get paid."

"We're cut from the same cloth, Ben. I already have calls in to both their parents. I'll get you Minnie and Morton."

"Then we have a deal."

Mr. Hecht and Charlie rise and shake hands.

***

Once again, Mr. Hecht is up and dressed and awaiting the delivery of the morning paper. Right on time the driver whizzes by and the paper lands at his feet.

Mr. Hecht opens it and pages through the first section. Sure enough, there's a full-page ad that reads, "High School and College Students: Want to work at a professional paper? *The Succotash Sentinel* is proud to announce the start of its Cub Reporter Program."

A smile comes across Mr. Hecht's face. This is nice. Very nice.

***

Mr. Hecht sits at his new desk in his new office at his new job at *The Succotash Sentinel*. It feels good to be back at a real newspaper.

The phone rings. Who could this be? It's the first hour of the first day. Does anyone even know he's there? He picks up the phone.

"Hecht here," he says with confidence.

It's been a long time since he answered a phone that way. In the old days his friends called him "Hecht Here," as if that were his name.

"Mr. Hecht," the voice says, "This is Dr. Hayes."

"What do *you* want?" he asks, not really caring to hear the answer.

"I had a discussion with the members of the school board and they — I — would like to offer you your job back at school."

Mr. Hecht is silent for a moment, just to let her wait. He already knows his decision, but he lets her wait.

"I'm very busy right now so I'm going to have to put you on hold," he says without emotion.

He doesn't press the hold button but hangs up the phone, never giving her another thought.

Chapter Ten

Once again — for the first time — Minnie walks into Mr. Hecht's classroom. Only this time it's not at Succotash Central High School, but at *The Succotash Sentinel*.

At this moment Minnie feels as if she's grown up a little. This is not a high school journalism class, but a real job at a real newspaper. She's no longer a scared, little girl on the first day of school but a paid reporter. And this time she's walking into the room hand-in-hand with Morton Damm.

There were a lot of changes in the past five weeks. The first day of school seems like a lifetime ago. Who knew so much could happen in such a short time?

"I guess that's what happens as you mature," deduces Minnie. "Time goes by more quickly and the changes are immense." Indeed it does and indeed they are.

There are a lot of familiar faces in the room. Christina Ambrico, Laura Bence and a few other old classmates. There are a lot of new faces, too, both girls and boys. Clearly the others are college students, many from Succotash Community College, or SCC.

But there's one face that doesn't seem right. Justin sits in a desk and when he sees Minnie and Morton walk in, he gives them a look of contempt and turns away.

Minnie and Morton glance at each other and take their seats as Mr. Hecht enters.

"Everyone is on time," he begins. "I like that. For those of you from the high school, I don't need to go over what we're doing. It's the same thing as there, only here.

"For the rest of you, we went over everything during your admissions interview. So there's no need to go over anything with you.

"All of you are here because you've demonstrated to me that you have potential as newspaper people. I expect you to treat it like a real job. Some of you are getting paid and some of you are getting college credit and the others are getting professional experience that you're not going to get at any school. In any case, this is your job now.

"Those of you from the high school are probably wondering why Justin is here." All the high school students nod their heads.

"Justin, why don't you tell them?"

"The Chief thinks I'm salvageable," he says. The class laughs.

"Yes, I do! I'm always up for a challenge so we'll see what happens."

Justin isn't thrilled to be Mr. Hecht's "challenge" but he's lucky to be there and he knows it. He also knows he needs to outshine Minnie and Morton and do it fast.

"Speaking of challenges," continues Mr. Hecht, "all of us have a challenge to take on right now. We need to have our first stories in the paper to be exceptional.

"There's only one first time for anything and we need to make our first time memorable. That means strong and compelling copy and pictures to match.

"I want at least one fervent profile piece and two robust news stories. Minnie's story is a tough act to follow... and that goes for Minnie, too." He turns to Minnie.

"Don't feel you have to top yourself. Don't go creating a story if there's not one there. Just keep doing what you did and the stories will come.

"The key to Minnie's success is she kept her eyes open and really looked at what's going on around her. The rest of you do the same. When we meet again the day after tomorrow I want to hear as many possible story ideas as you can come up with."

***

Most men want a son. Some of them like doing "guy stuff" and want a son to do it with. Others think they have to "carry on the family name" for some reason and a son does that job.

Mr. Mornap is not like most men. When he found out his wife was expecting, he secretly hoped for a girl. And when Minnie was born, it was one of the greatest days of his life.

Mr. and Mrs. Mornap weren't supposed to be able to conceive. Mrs. Mornap has a medical condition which was supposed to prevent this from happening.

Sometimes doctors are wrong — or miracles happen — but whichever was the case Minnie was born to what was supposed to be a childless couple.

Mr. Mornap would love to go through it again... and again... and have three daughters but he has to be happy with just one. He's indeed happy because Minnie is the center of his world. She'll always be Daddy's Little Girl.

Both Mr. and Mrs. Mornap know just how lucky they are. Some children turn out to be a big disappointment. Minnie is no disappointment but quite the opposite. She brings great joy to them both.

Minnie's article in the paper thrilled them, especially Mr. Mornap. How did Daddy's Little Girl pull off such an achievement? They know Mr. Hecht had a lot to do with it but even so, it's really something for her to do.

Upon their return from Africa, when they learned of the recent events at the school, they immediately planned two things: The first was to see Dr. Hayes to both set the story straight and scream at her so hard her head would spin.

Mr. Mornap isn't the type to scream at people but he was so livid he felt justified this time. Unfortunately, the superintendent knew what was going to happen so she didn't return his calls and they never met. He never had the opportunity to set the story straight or to scream at her.

The other thing he did with ease. He bought Minnie a police scanner. If investigative reporting was her talent, then she needed the tools to succeed and a police scanner is one of those tools.

Minnie was thrilled to receive it and she put it in her room, on the nightstand next to her bed, and keeps it on all night. Maybe Mr. Turner isn't so crazy.

Not that she could go to a crime scene in the middle of the night. At 15 she doesn't drive yet. But her 16th birthday is March sixth, so she'll be able to sign up for driver's ed in the spring. With the weeks flying by faster and faster, her birthday will be here soon enough.

If her article about the principal got her a scanner, what would she have to write for her parents to buy her a car?

***

"The day after tomorrow" arrived rather quickly.

"Lemme hear 'em!" exclaims Mr. Hecht. To both his surprise and his liking, several hands are in the air immediately.

"Theresa. You're new here. You go first."

Theresa is from the community college so she's much older than Minnie and her friends. She's quite beautiful with thick, dark hair and pale skin. Her full eyebrows and brown eyes are accentuated against her pastel skin.

"In school, we're required to buy textbooks for our classes. Some of these books are over $100. And many of them are written by the professors teaching the classes.

"In a math class last year, we had to buy the book at the beginning of the fall semester and then buy the 'revised edition' at the beginning of the spring semester! The only thing revised about it was the price."

"Are these books available in electronic form?" asks Minnie.

How Mr. Hecht loves Minnie. It's precisely what he's thinking.

"No, they're not. That would save us a lot of money but not one is an e-book."

"I know where you're going with this," says Mr. Hecht. "Tell the class what you're thinking."

"I'm thinking these professors have a racket going. They write the books. We buy the books and then we have to buy them again."

"Sounds that way to me," says Mr. Hecht. "Go ahead and get on this. I think you have a story here. OK, who's next?"

Minnie has her hand up.

"*Minnie*...." says Mr. Hecht, in a way that says he's expecting something exceptional.

"I hear the Succotash Museum of Art and Antiquities is getting an exhibit of ancient Egyptian art, on loan from the Cairo Museum. I'd love to do something with that."

"Oh, you would?" asks Mr. Hecht, sarcastically. He stares at her for a moment with a smirk on his face.

He opens his desk drawer and produces four press passes.

"It just so happens the museum already gave me four press passes to the reception. I was planning on giving one to you and one to Morton."

He hands one to each of them. He holds the third one in the air.

"I'm keeping one," as he places it back in his drawer, "and that leaves one more —"

Before he can say another word everyone's hand is in the air as they shout for the last pass.

"Calm down," says Mr. Hecht. "I already made up my mind I'm giving the last one to Justin."

Justin?! What is he thinking?

"Justin, here's your chance," says Mr. Hecht, as he hands him the fourth and last pass. "I'm giving you an opportunity to do some real reportage. Are you up for it?"

"Sure thing, Chief," says Justin.

"Before the three of you leave this evening, I need to tell you a few things about the exhibit so stick around."

***

The "class" or whatever it is Mr. Hecht is going to call this group — he's not sure — has dispersed except for Minnie, Morton and Justin.

"Has it struck any of you as odd that this exhibit is coming here, to the Succotash Valley?" asks Mr. Hecht.

"When the King Tutankahem exhibit first came to America in the 1970s, it was at the Metropolitan Museum of Art in New York City. Then when it came around again in 2007 it was at the Franklin Institute in Philadelphia."

"So why isn't this new exhibit at one of those places or at the National Gallery in D.C.?" asks Minnie.

"That's the very question I had," answers Mr. Hecht, sort of. "It seems none of those places wanted it."

"Why not?" asks Justin.

"Well... it appears these artifacts... are cursed."

The three don't know if this is a joke or not.

"Now I don't believe in curses or any hocus pocus but there are a lot of people who do. And if some of those people are running major museums and they're too scared to host this exhibit, well then that's news and news worth reporting.

"If there's a story here — and I think there is — your job is to find it. Start digging."

Chapter Eleven

Minnie, Morton and Justin stand outside *The Succotash Sentinel* building waiting for their ride.

"This having-to-get-picked-up-and-dropped-off business is sure getting old," thinks Minnie. Her 16th birthday isn't getting here fast enough.

It's a balmy evening in the Succotash Valley. Balmy is Minnie's favorite weather, yet there are only two or three balmy days a year.

She never really understood what's going on weather-wise when it's balmy, and no one could give her a useful answer when she asked, so it's all a big mystery to her.

Nevertheless, it's balmy right now and she's loving it. She's also loving standing next to Morton.

What she's not loving is Justin is standing there, too, almost right on top of them. There's an awkward silence that Minnie can no longer tolerate.

"I just love balmy weather," says Minnie, to no one in particular.

There's another intolerable period of awkward silence.

Minnie looks at her press pass. "It was awfully nice of the Chief to give us these press passes. Makes me feel like a real reporter."

More silence.

"Will one of you say something?!" screams Minnie inside her head.

It's Justin who comes to her rescue.

"I believe it," he states.

Minnie and Morton aren't sure what he's referring to.

"The curse. I believe that stuff is cursed."

He's talking about the ancient Egyptian artifacts.

"For real?" asks Morton.

"If all those museums turned down the exhibit, then there must be something to it," he argues.

"I'm not buying it," is Morton's only retort. Looking for an ally, he asks, "What do you think, Minnie?"

"I'm not sure."

Not the answer Morton was looking for.

"The Chief said for us to start digging. I've got an idea."

***

Mrs. Mornap's SUV pulls up in front of the Succotash Museum of Art and Antiquities. Minnie, Morton and Justin spill out onto the sidewalk. Mrs. Mornap, being a very smart mom, stays in the car and will wait for them.

The trio enters the building and approaches the information desk, where a white-haired, old lady is seated. She looks like she's as old as the antiquities the museum displays.

"Hello, children."

Not one of them likes being called a child.

"The museum closes at eight o'clock and it's nearly eight now," she states.

"We don't want to see the museum," begins Minnie. "We're from Succotash High — I mean

The Succotash Sentinel — and we'd like to see the museum director."

"It's awfully late…." the white-haired lady begins.

"I'm the museum director," says a voice from a few feet away.

Everyone turns to see the museum director who doesn't look much like a museum director. Although she wears a brown pantsuit — which is what one would expect an administrator to wear — handmade, ceramic peace signs hang from a beaded necklace.

Handcrafted hoops made of silver dangle from her ears. Clearly this "suit" is a leftover hippie. A mood ring would complete the ensemble.

She extends her hand to Minnie. She wears a mood ring.

"I'm Sarah Fadil. Pleased to meet you."

"I'm Minnie Mornap and this is Morton Damm and Justin Hearst. We're all reporters from *The Succotash Sentinel*."

Each shakes hands with Sarah.

"We'd like to ask you a few questions about the Egyptian exhibit," says Minnie.

"You're in luck," says Sarah. "The liaison from Cairo is in my office right now. You can meet him if you'd like."

"What a stroke of good luck!" thinks Minnie. But all she says is, "Sure."

They arrive at Sarah's office. There's no door but a curtain made of beads. One by one they part the beads and enter the office which looks more like a dorm room at Berkley circa 1968.

Colored, silk scarves set atop the lampshades, emitting soft, pastel colors in all directions. An aquarium of exotic fish adds to the pallet of endless colors. A huge parrot squawks his "hello" from an even bigger cage. Meticulously crafted bonsai plants adorn the tabletops.

Once they're finished taking in the eclectic décor of the room, Minnie, Morton and Justin see the liaison, whose back is to them. He's busy perusing the reference books in the bookcase. He turns around.

"This is Anwar Kek, the liaison from the Cairo Museum. These are reporters from *The Succotash Sentinel*."

"My pleasure," says Anwar in his Egyptian accent as he bows ever so slightly.

"Pull up some chairs and have a seat," instructs Sarah. Everyone does.

"Ask your questions," says Sarah to Minnie from behind her desk.

Minnie is about to speak when Morton holds up his index finger. He reaches into his pocket and produces his digital recorder. He presses "record" and sets the thing atop Sarah's desk. Morton nods to Minnie.

"We've been told that all the other museums turned down this exhibit because it's cursed. Is it safe to assume you don't believe in curses?"

Sarah laughs. "I believe in lots of things that most people think is a load of snake oil. Transcendental meditation, karma — things people in the West tend to dismiss — but there's one thing I *don't* believe in and that's curses. That's why I've signed a contract to bring the exhibit here. It's a done deal."

Minnie turns to Anwar. "Do *you* believe in curses?"

"What I believe in is not important. But what my ancestors believed in is. My people had an understanding of the afterlife and the spirits who dwell there. To them curses were very real. To them, they *are* very real."

"This is getting a little spooky," thinks Minnie. She presses on.

"Why are these artifacts cursed?"

"Most everything in this exhibit was buried with a pharaoh, a high priest or someone else of great stature. These items were intended to aid their spirits in their journey to the afterlife.

"They were not intended to be looted from the burial sites, as so many were over the centuries. My people knew the possibility of looters, so they cursed the items to bring great hardship to those who disturbed the sacred burial sites."

Just then the bird starts squawking and fluttering his wings almost uncontrollably. No one knows what to make of this. He settles down after a few seconds.

Now Morton and Justin are spooked. Morton reaches into his bag and produces his camera. "Do you think I can get a picture of the two of you?"

"Great idea!" says a relieved Minnie.

"Come with me to the floor that will hold the exhibit. That'll make a good picture," says Sarah.

Morton retrieves his recorder as they file out of the room.

The five of them walk up the stairs to the second floor with Sarah leading the way. When she opens the fire door Minnie lets out a yelp.

The other four turn to her. She points to the floor as a beetle scurries across their path.

Anwar mumbles something in Egyptian under his breath.

"Oh, my," says Sarah. "That's never happened before. I better call an exterminator."

They step into the gallery. Ordinarily the walls are painted white but now they're painted beiges and browns in keeping with Egyptian desert motif.

Wooden crates of all sizes are scattered about. Some of them have the lids pried open while others are still sealed tight. Ladders, pry bars and other tools lay around the room with no particular arrangement.

"As you can see, the artifacts have arrived from Cairo and we're just about ready to install the exhibit. The first pieces will be hung tomorrow," says Sarah.

"Let me get a shot of the two of you standing near some crates," says Morton.

Sarah and Anwar follow his direction. As Morton knocks off a few pictures, his flash firing with each, the air is pierced with a shriek far louder and penetrating than Minnie's previous one.

Once again they turn to Minnie. A look of terror paralyzes her face. All she can do is point to the floor.

They turn and look at the floor. Hundreds upon hundreds of beetles scurry in all directions. The place is crawling with them.

Everyone hightails it to the stairs. Everyone except Anwar. He drops to his knees and kowtows towards the crates. With arms outstretched forwardly, he touches his head to the floor and prays in Egyptian.

Morton's photojournalist's instincts kick in and he steps back into the room and fires off a few more pictures of Anwar (and the beetles) before he retreats.

In the temporary "safety" of the stairwell, Minnie, Morton, Justin and Sarah look at each other in disbelief.

Minnie turns to Justin. "I think you're right. These artifacts *are* cursed."

Minnie's deductive reasoning came to that conclusion extremely fast. But was it too fast?

Ordinarily Justin would be thrilled to hear he's finally right about something but he's just too freaked out to shower in self-glory.

Minnie steps towards the fire door. She opens it a crack and looks into the gallery. Anwar is still on his knees, praying. The beetles are still scurrying across the floor.

"Yes," Minnie says quietly. "These artifacts *are* cursed."

To Be Continued

Be sure to read Book 2 *in the* Minnie Mornap, Teen Reporter *series called* The Pharaoh's Curse *to see what happens next.*

Printed in the United States
By Bookmasters